The Travellers

The first book:
Tess's story

The second book:
Mike's story

The third book:
Lizzie's story

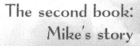

The Travellers: Tess
by Rosemary Hayes

Published by Ransom Publishing Ltd.
Unit 7, Brocklands Farm, West Meon, Hampshire GU32 1JN, UK
www.ransom.co.uk

ISBN   978 178127 967 0
First published in 2015

Tess

The first book in the series

Rosemary Hayes

Ransom

Acknowledgements

My thanks to everyone who has made time to tell me about the lives of Gypsy/Romany/Travellers, how they live now and how they lived in the past, particularly to those in Cambridgeshire County Council who work with the GRT community and to Gordon Boswell of The Romany Museum, Spalding, Lincolnshire.

I am very grateful to the following members of GRT families who have welcomed me into their homes and talked to me about their experiences:

Brady
Linda
Andrew
Rene
Jessie
Abraham
Abi
and Rita.

The English gypsies I spoke to referred to themselves as either gypsies or travellers, and these terms appear to be interchangeable. Many have Romany roots and still practise some of the old traditions and use words from the Romany language.

Traveller Organisations

The Community Law Partnership (CLP) incorporates the Travellers' Advice Team, a nationwide 24-hour advice service for gypsies and travellers.

The National Federation of Gypsy Liaison Groups

The Gypsy Council

Friends, Families and Travellers

National Association of Gypsy and Traveller Officers

Travellers' Times

One

It was raining hard. Tess's mum, Kate, got out of the car and put up her umbrella. Tess ducked underneath it and they ran up the path to the village hall.

Even before they reached the door they could hear angry, shouting voices.

The hall was packed and Kate and Tess squeezed through the door and stood at the back, jammed against a load of other people. It was hot and stuffy and Tess banged her elbows into someone as she shrugged off her school blazer and slung it over her arm.

A woman was standing at the front of the hall, behind a table. 'Can we have quiet, *please*,' she said.

But the noise just got louder.

Someone shouted. 'You never asked us about this. You've gone behind our backs.'

There was a roar from the crowd, then a man in front of Tess, with a shaved head and a thick neck, cupped his hands over his mouth and yelled: 'Yeah, right! No one asked us. We don't want no filthy gypsies round here! End of.'

Tess looked round the room. She recognised a few people. There were some of the staff from the technical college where Mum worked as a receptionist, and she saw Mr Hardy, the headteacher from her school, pushing his way through the crowd to the front.

'This is chaotic,' muttered Kate. 'The council have got a real fight on their hands.'

Mr Hardy was at the front, now. He stood up on a chair and clapped his hands.

Everyone knew him. He'd been teaching at the primary school for years. Gradually, the noise in the room died down.

Mr Hardy pointed to the people sitting at the table beside him. 'Let's hear what the councillors have to say,' he said. 'There'll be plenty of time for questions later.'

'Too right there'll be questions!'

'We don't want gypsies in this village.'

Mr Hardy clapped his hands together again. Tess had seen him at school assemblies, getting the kids' attention, quietening them down. He was doing the same thing here, as if all these grown-ups were primary-school children.

'Right,' said Mr Hardy, as the people settled down. 'Please listen to the councillors.' He held up his hand again, as there was more muttering. 'You'll have your say later.'

Mr Hardy stepped down and a man in a suit stood up behind the table. He fiddled with the papers in his hands, adjusted his specs on his nose and smoothed the few remaining hairs over his shiny bald head.

Tess yawned and zoned out as he spoke about the wasteland where the council had created a site for travellers under the motorway bridge, and how it was important to welcome them into the village community … etc. etc.

Boring, boring, boring. Tess looked at her watch.

How long was this going to drag on? She took out her phone and checked her messages. One from Sophie and another from Tara, both with silly selfies. She giggled out loud and her mum nudged her and frowned.

Tess texted back. At v hall. Boring or what?

At last the councillor stopped speaking and at once the noise started up again. Once more, Mr Hardy climbed on the chair.

'We'll have one question at a time.'

A whole lot of people raised their hands. Mr Hardy pointed at a woman who worked with Tess's mum.

'The site may be some way from the village,' she said, 'but it's very close to the technical college.'

'What's your point?' asked Mr Hardy. Tess recognised the anger in his voice. She'd heard him speak like that to some of the cheeky little sods in the playground.

The woman cleared her throat. 'Well, I'm just saying that the site may not affect the main village so much, but it could have an impact on the college.'

'In what way, exactly?'

The woman was floundering. 'Well … '

'She's talking about thieving,' shouted someone.

'Thieving and litter and mess. These people live like animals.'

Kate gasped. 'That's a dreadful thing to say,' she whispered to Tess, and for a moment the remark seemed to stun everyone in the hall, but then someone else shouted out: 'Yeah, and they'll have a whole lot of dogs with them. What about if the dogs get loose and bite people?'

More voices were raised. 'And cock fighting. I've heard they do that, too. That's really cruel.'

'And horses,' shouted someone else. 'They're bound to have horses. And you'll bet they won't look after them properly, poor things.'

Tess raised her head and snapped her phone shut. Horses? These people had horses? She stopped listening and started to daydream about owning a pony and becoming a top show jumper.

The angry shouting got louder, but Tess didn't hear; she was too busy thinking about ponies.

Then suddenly the room went silent and Tess felt Kate clutch her arm.

'Oh no,' said Kate. 'That's awful!'

'What?'

'Weren't you listening? They're here.'

'Who?'

'One of the families who are going to live at the

site. The councillor's just introduced them. They've been here all along, listening to all this stuff people have been saying about them.'

'Where are they?'

'There. Right there out at the front.'

They'd been sitting unnoticed amongst the crowd of people and now they'd been asked to come and stand at the front. It was as if the whole room was shrinking from them. People pushed their chairs back, so that the space at the front was larger, leaving them standing there exposed, facing the village.

A mother and father, an older boy of around 15 or so, several smaller children and a girl who looked about 10 – Tess's age. They stood there, the adults looking at their feet, the smaller children clinging onto their mother's skirt.

Tess stared at them. She'd never thought about how a gypsy family would look. Until today she'd hardly heard of gypsies – *travellers* – but they didn't look that different from the other people in the hall. They certainly weren't dirty or anything. The woman wore lots of bracelets, gold hooped earrings and a dress, unlike most of the other women in the hall who were wearing jeans, and the man had a sort of medallion round his neck and some gold rings. But other than that, they looked – well, *normal*.

Mr Hardy went up to them, shaking hands with the adults and older children and squatting down to talk to the little children. Then he stood up and faced the crowded room.

'These people will be our neighbours,' he said. 'I hope you will make them welcome.'

There was an embarrassed silence. Then the father of the family nodded to Mr Hardy and started walking towards the door. The rest of his family followed him.

Tess was close to the door of the hall as the traveller family filed out. As she was staring at them, the older girl suddenly raised her head and looked straight at Tess; for a moment their eyes met.

She's really pretty, thought Tess, taking in the girl's curly dark hair and big eyes. *Perhaps she'll be at our school next term.*

Once the family had left, the talking began again, not quite so loud, but no less hostile.

Tess tugged on Kate's sleeve. 'Can we go now, Mum?'

'Well, I thought I'd speak to … '

'*Mum*, it's late and I've got homework!'

That got Kate's attention.

'Oh ... oh, all right. I think I've heard enough.'

It had stopped raining when they left the hall. On the way back to the car Tess said, 'Why was everyone so horrible about that family?'

Kate shrugged. 'Well, travellers don't have a great reputation,' she said.

'Is it true, then, what those people were saying – about stealing and treating animals badly and being dirty?'

'I don't know, love, but ... '

'But what?'

Kate sighed. 'I'm not sure I'd trust them.'

Tess remembered a book she'd had when she was little, with pictures of painted wooden caravans drawn by skewbald and piebald horses.

'Do they live in wagons?'

'I doubt it. Not now. I think they live in either caravans or houses.'

'But they still have the horses? Someone there said they had horses.'

Kate had reached the car. She climbed into the driver's seat and put on her seat belt, as Tess scrambled into the passenger seat.

'Do they, Mum? Do they have horses?'

'Oh for heaven's sake, Tess, how should I know?'

'Perhaps I could … ?'

Kate turned quickly. 'I know what you are thinking, Tess, and the answer is no. Don't you *dare* even think of it! You keep well away from the gypsies, do you hear?'

She put the keys into the ignition and started the car.

'What *is* it with you and horses?' she muttered, as she reversed the car, did a U-turn and headed for home.

They didn't speak on the way back. When they reached their house, the lights were blazing.

'Oh good, Ben's home,' said Kate.

Tess came back down to earth. She'd been imagining living in a big house with its own paddocks and stables, and winning trophies and masses of rosettes with her very own beautiful pony.

She sighed as she gathered up her school bag and followed Kate inside their front door. In the real world, things were very different. Tess lived in a council house on the outskirts of a boring village. Her Dad didn't live with them and Ben was a pain.

Ben was in the lounge, sprawling on the settee watching some noisy DVD.

'Turn it down, Ben,' Kate yelled.

'Hello to you, too, Mum,' said Ben.

Kate took off her jacket. She went over to Ben and ruffled his hair. How was the footie practice?'

Ben squirmed away from her. 'Orright,' he muttered.

'Sorry we're late,' said Kate. 'We've been at the meeting about the travellers' site down by the college.'

Ben abandoned his game for a second. 'Scum,' he said.

'Ben!'

'Well, they'll only be trouble, won't they? They're just a bunch of thieves.'

But they'll have horses, thought Tess. *Lucky things.*

Two

Tess was sitting in the school yard at break time with her friends, Sophie and Tara. The sun was beating down on them and Sophie took a swig from her bottle of water.

'Only one more week of term,' she said, wiping the moisture from her lip.

'Summer holidays – yay!' Tara punched the air.

Tess said nothing. The long weeks of boredom stretched ahead. It was all right for Sophie and

Tara, they would be going on fancy holidays with their families. It was different for her.

Sophie combed her fingers through her long fair hair and pushed some stray curls behind her ears. 'You doing anything special, Tess?'

Tess shook her head. 'I suppose I'll have to see Dad and Emma,' she said, scuffing her shoe on the ground.

Sophie and Tara started talking about their holiday plans and Tess stopped listening. Instead she thought about Dad and Emma and their new baby. She didn't want to visit. Although they were nice enough to her, it always felt awkward. She didn't fit into Dad's new life.

Tara nudged her. 'Hey. I asked you a question.'

Tess came back to earth. 'Sorry.'

'So, what was this thing you were at last night?'

Tess dragged her thoughts back to the present. 'It was about the gypsies coming to the village,' she said.

'God, yes, I've heard about them. Everyone's really worried,' said Tara.

'They've been stealing stuff already,' said Sophie.

Tess frowned as she remembered the face of the dark-haired gypsy girl and how, for a moment, their eyes had met. 'What stuff?' she asked.

Sophie shrugged. 'Oh I dunno, there's been things going missing from garden sheds and that.'

'How do they know it's gypsies stealing it? It could be anyone.'

Sophie raised her eyebrows.

Tess turned on her. 'It could. Just because they're different … '

'OK, OK, cool it, Tess.'

But Tess wouldn't leave it. 'You're the same as all those people last night. It was horrible. That poor family.'

'There was a gypsy family there, at the meeting?'

Tess nodded. 'No one realised. They walked out in the end.'

The bell rang and the girls trooped back inside. Just as they reached the door of their classroom, Mr Hardy walked past, his arms full of books. He stopped when he saw Tess.

'You and your mum were at the meeting last night, Tess, weren't you?' he said.

Tess blushed and nodded.

'There'll be some travelling children in Year Six next term,' he said. Then he turned to the others.

'I hope I can rely on all of you to make them welcome.'

'Yes, Mr Hardy,' they chorused.

'He's going to be our form teacher next term, isn't he?' whispered Sophie to Tess as they took their seats.

All through the next lesson, Tess couldn't concentrate. She was thinking of the gypsy girl. She'd be in their class next term.

For the first week of the summer holidays, Sophie and Tara were still around and Tess hung out with them. They went to each others' houses or rode round the village on their bikes. For most of the time, Tess forgot about the travellers but one day, as the girls were sitting on the swings in the rec, chatting, she saw a horsebox going down the street. She stood up and watched as it headed along the road which led to the college. The road didn't go anywhere else; it ended at the gypsy site under the motorway bridge.

'They're taking horses there!' she said.

Tara was sitting on one of the swings. 'Where? What are you on about?'

Tess pointed. 'That horsebox. It's going to the site.'

Sophie groaned. 'What is it with you and horses, Tess? You're obsessed.'

Tess took no notice. 'I want to go and see,' she said.

'What?'

She nodded. 'I want to go and see where they keep the horses.'

'You're nuts,' said Tara.

Tess pushed Tara off the swing. 'Come on. Let's go.'

'No way,' said Tara. 'I'm not going to some poxy gypsy site.'

Tess went over to her bike and started to mount it. 'OK, I'll go on my own then.'

'No wait. Don't be stupid, Tess. You don't know what … '

Tess scowled at her. 'What? You think I'll be attacked or something? You're as bad as the rest of them.' She pushed down on the pedals and began to ride away.

Sophie and Tara looked at each other and shrugged. Then they got on their bikes and followed Tess out of the rec and down the road out of the village that led to the site.

'Wait, Tess!' shouted Sophie. 'We're coming.'

Tess waited for them to catch up and they biked in single file down the road past the technical college. She glanced nervously towards the main entrance, knowing that her mum was working there.

The road narrowed as it went under the motorway bridge and then suddenly they were there.

'It's all changed,' said Tara. 'I came here once and it was horrible; a real tip.'

Tess looked around. It was true. There was no sign of rubbish now and the site looked clean and tidy. There was a small road going through it and on either side of the road there were big caravans, each surrounded by a patch of land. There were some new houses, too, with ordinary yards, some with washing lines with clothes flapping in the breeze.

Suddenly a dog barked and they heard a man shouting at it.

Tara jumped. 'Come on,' she said, turning her bike round. 'We don't want them to see us. Let's go.'

But Tess hesitated. 'Where do they keep the horses?'

'Tess!' said Sophie. 'Come *on!*'

Slowly, Tess turned her bike round, but she didn't get on. She pushed it in front of her, looking round all the time. As she passed a small lane, she suddenly stopped.

'Look! Let's go down there. I bet that goes round

the back of the site to a field. That's where they'll keep the horses.'

Without waiting for the others, Tess pushed her bike down the lane. There were high hedges on either side.

Tara and Sophie followed her, looking nervously around.

'No one can see us,' said Tess.

'But Sophie hesitated. 'I don't like it, Tess. Let's go back.'

Tess didn't answer. She tried to mount her bike but the lane was too overgrown and bumpy. She threw the bike on the ground and ran on down the lane.

She was right. The lane led to the back of the site and then stopped at a gate into a field.

And there they were. There must have been ten or- twelve ponies, heavy cobs, some black and white, some brown and white. And among them one lighter, chestnut pony.

As Tess climbed onto the gate and gripped the top bar, the chestnut pony raised its head and whinnied.

There was no one in the field with them and Tess stared, transfixed, until Sophie and Tara caught up with her, panting with the effort.

'OK. You've seen your dumb horses, Tess. Come on, before someone spots us.' She took Tess's arm and pulled at it.

Tess sighed and the three of them made their way back into the village.

Three

That night, Tess dreamt about the ponies at the site. In her dream, she was riding the chestnut pony, galloping down a long stretch of sand beside the sea. When she woke up, she was still thinking about them.

The next week, Tara and Sophie went on holiday with their families. Tess stayed at home. Kate only worked part-time in the holidays, and when she wasn't at home she made Ben look after Tess.

'Why do I have to babysit her?' said Ben. 'She's such a pain.'

'*I* don't want you to,' snapped Tess. 'I'd much rather be on my own.'

Kate looked tired.

'Look, I'd love to be with you here, but I have to work some of the time. There are conferences at the college in the summer. They need me there.'

Ben and Tess shut up then. But the truce didn't last long and soon they were quarrelling so much that Kate packed Tess off to a holiday club for a few days and then, in the second week of the holidays, she sent her off to visit her dad.

'Oh Mum, do I have to?'

Kate nodded. 'You see little enough of him. And there's the baby. You'll like helping with the baby … '

Tess looked up sharply and met Kate's eyes. She knew Mum was really upset about Dad's new baby. Perhaps she was thinking of the times when she and Dad were happy, when Ben and she were babies. Before everything had gone wrong.

Kate drove Tess to Dad's house. It was a long journey, and by the time they arrived Kate was tired and grumpy. She heaved Tess's backpack out of the car and they walked up the path to the house. Tess looked at the neat garden. Nothing out of place. Rather like Dad's new wife, Emma. She always looked neat and tidy.

Emma opened the door, the baby on her hip. Tess looked from her to Mum. Emma was tall, and her height made Mum look even smaller – and Tess like a midget. Mum was wearing jeans and a crumpled shirt and her dark hair fell over her eyes. Emma, as always, looked as though she'd just walked out of a fashion show.

How does she do it? thought Tess. *With a new baby and everything?*

Just then, Dad loomed up behind Emma and put a hand on her shoulder. Emma moved aside and Dad came forward.

'Hi love. Great to see you.' He gave Tess a big hug.

'Hi Kate,' he said. He took Tess's backpack from her, but they didn't touch.

They all went inside and had a cup of tea. Emma had baked a perfect cake and, despite herself, Tess ate two slices, but the atmosphere was awkward. The adults made stilted conversation and all the time the baby, who they'd called Tom, crawled around the floor. At one point, Dad picked him up and hugged him and then put him on Tess's lap. Tom tugged at her nose and Tess laughed, the tension easing for a moment. But then Tess looked up and saw the hurt in her mum's eyes.

'I'd best be going,' said Kate, swallowing the last of her cup of tea. 'Long journey ahead of me.'

She kissed Tess goodbye and headed out of the door. As Tess watched her go, she suddenly felt a wrench in her gut. She waved.

'See you soon, Mum. Drive carefully.'

Tess only saw Dad in the evenings. The rest of the time she was cooped up with Emma and baby Tom. Although Emma was always nice to Tess, she never seemed natural with her. Sometimes Tess wanted her to yell, admit she was fed up with having her, but they both skirted around one another. Walking on eggshells.

The only relief was the time Tess spent with little Tom. He seemed to love her without any reservation, stretching out his pudgy arms to her when she came into the room, laughing until he had hiccups when she played with him.

One evening, Dad and Tess were alone. Emma had gone to bed early.

'How are things at home, Tess?' said Dad.

Tess looked down at her hands. 'Fine,' she mumbled. She wasn't about to tell him how bored she was, how fed up she was with Ben.

'Really?'

'Yes, really.' Suddenly she was angry with him. *He'd* chosen to leave them, hadn't he? It was none of his business, anyway.

There was an awkward silence, then Dad said something really unexpected.

'I feel I don't know you any more, Tess. What do you want? What makes you happy?'

Tess burst out. 'I want to ride. I want a pony.'

Where did that come from?

Dad laughed out loud – and she hated him for it.

'*A pony!* Get real, love. That's not going to happen, is it?'

Of course it wasn't going to happen. She lived in a council house. Mum struggled to earn enough money to pay the rent and pay the bills. Of course she wasn't going to have a pony!

Tess got up and turned to face him. She was near to tears. 'No, of course it's not going to happen. Do you think I don't know that? But you asked me what I want and that's what I want.'

Then she ran out of the room, slamming the

door so hard behind her that the whole house shuddered.

The days dragged. Emma took Tess to the park a few times with Tom in his buggy, but mostly they stayed in the house, trying not to get in each other's way.

'It's a shame I can't go out with you, Tess, but with the baby ... '

'It's OK, I understand.'

Why had Mum made her come? They tried to make her feel welcome, but it was obvious they didn't want her.

At last, Mum came to fetch her. Dad was at work when she came.

Tess gave Emma a peck on the cheek, then she picked up Tom and gave him a hug.

'Bye, little man,' she whispered.

She looked back as they got into the car and saw Tom stretching out his arms towards her, trying to reach her. Kate was busy driving off into the traffic and Tess thought she hadn't noticed, but she had.

'He's a lovely baby,' she said, her voice flat.

Something about Kate's bleak tone made Tess turn. She put a hand on Kate's knee.

'Yes,' she said softly. 'But he was the only good thing about the visit.'

Four

When Tess got back from her dad's, Sophie and Tara had returned from their holidays. All the time they'd been away, Tess had had texts and photos from them. Their holiday photos looked fantastic: sun and sand and watersports.

The next day, Tess set off for Sophie's house as usual, but suddenly she couldn't face any more holiday chat. She got off her bike and stood beside it in the road for a moment, then she turned it round, got back on and pedalled off in the direction of the Tech.

At first, she wasn't sure what she was going to do. Mum was only working in the morning and Tess had told Ben she'd be at Sophie's. He'd been nicer to her since the girls came back and he'd been freer to do his own thing and see his own friends. He'd grinned as she'd left the house.

'Another girly day?'

She had stuck out her tongue at him as she'd biked off.

Her heart thumped in her chest as she rode quickly past the Tech and on down the road that ended in the site. There was no one about as she hid her bike in the hedge and walked cautiously down the lane until she reached the gate. But then she drew back quickly.

The ponies were all there, just as before, but today there were a couple of boys in with them. They were older than her – probably more Ben's age. One was grooming a skewbald pony. The pony was tied loosely to the fence at the far side of the field and Tess could hear the boy whistling as he brushed. The other boy was filling a water trough with a hose.

Hidden behind the hedge, Tess watched them. She recognised the boy grooming the pony. He had dark slicked back hair and was stockily built. He'd been at that meeting in the village hall and she wondered if he was the brother of the girl she seen there, the one who'd stared at her.

Then suddenly one of the ponies raised its head, whinnied and cantered towards where Tess was hidden.

She stood completely still, willing the boys not to come over. The boy with the hose looked up briefly, but he didn't move. He just wiped his nose with the back of his hand and went on filling the trough.

But Tess didn't want to be caught snooping, so she crept away, back to the start of the lane and jumped on her bike. When she was just past the Tech, she heard her phone ping. She stopped and took it out of her pocket. A message from Sophie.

Where are u?

On my way.

Tess didn't tell her friends she'd been to the site. She knew what they'd say, but all morning she thought about the ponies, and by the time she went home, she knew she'd go again.

After that, every time she left the house telling Mum – or Ben – she was off to see Sophie or Tara, it wasn't a lie. She *would* see them, but not until she'd made her daily visit to the ponies in the field behind the site.

She started taking food, carrots from the vegetable drawer in the fridge or apples from the fruit bowl, carefully cut up into segments.

It wasn't long before the ponies recognised her and came trotting over to the gate, pushing each other out of the way to get the food, nudging Tess's pockets. Tess studied them carefully. They all had different characters. Most of them were black and white or brown and white cobs, stocky, with long manes and tails and long hairs over their feet. Tess made a fuss of them all and had her own names for them.

But the chestnut mare was the one she specially liked. She was of a lighter build then the rest and her coat gleamed in the sunlight. Tess called her Flame.

Sometimes, Tess would see the two boys in the field, but she was always careful to hide until they went away.

Then one morning, as Tess had just got off her bike, she heard a shout and before she had time to hide, two ponies came thundering down the lane towards her, ridden bareback by the two boys she'd seen in the field.

The ponies were startled by her and they slithered to a halt and snorted, almost unseating their riders.

They were barring her path. Tess couldn't move.

One of the boys turned to the other and said something like 'gorger girl'.

Tess looked up at them, too scared to talk. She blushed, not knowing what to say.

Then one of the boys slipped off his pony's back to the ground. He was so close beside her that she could see the oil on his slicked back hair and was aware of his grimy hands loosely holding the rope of the halter. Tess shrank away from him, back into the hedge. For a moment the boy said nothing, just stared at her, and Tess could feel her heart beating furiously in her chest.

Then he looked back at his friend and they started talking and laughing, but she couldn't understand what they said. They spoke so fast and she didn't recognise some of the words they used. Some they repeated and she heard them say 'cushti', 'gry' and 'gorger' several times, but she had no idea what they meant.

They showed no sign of moving away, and when the boy on the ground turned back to her and said something, she didn't understand him. He repeated himself, speaking more slowly this time.

'You bin feeding the ponies?'

Tess swallowed. 'Sorry,' she said. 'I didn't mean any harm.'

Why won't the ground just swallow me up? Why did I ever come down here? What an idiot.

He grinned then, a slow smile spreading over his face.

'We've bin watching you,' he said.

Tess started to tremble. How often had they seen her feeding the ponies, talking to them, calling them by the names she'd invented for them?

'It's OK, girl,' said the boy. 'We don't mind.'

Tess was so flustered she didn't take in what he was saying. 'I'm sorry,' she said again.

'You like horses?'

Tess was close to tears. She nodded, not trusting herself to speak.

Just then, his pony put its head down to crop at the grass and automatically Tess started to stroke its neck.

The boy patted the pony. 'She's a nice mare, this one. We should get a good price for her.'

Tess looked up at last. 'You're selling her?' she whispered.

The boy nodded. 'Yeah. Dad does a bit of horse trading.'

The other boy was sitting astride his pony, his legs dangling, watching.

'Give her a ride, Mike,' he said suddenly.

Tess thought she would stop breathing. Did he mean it? Would they really let her?

Mike grinned. 'You heard what Johnny said. You want a go?'

Tess nodded.

Mike flung the rope round the pony's neck and knotted it onto the other side of the halter.

''Ere, I'll give you a leg up.'

He gave her such a heave that she almost slid off the other side of the pony's back.

'Skinny kid, ain't you? Hang onto the rope and grip with yer knees.

Johnny wheeled his pony round and rode back up the lane towards the field. Mike ran beside Tess, occasionally shouting encouragement as her pony broke into a trot.

But Tess needed no encouragement. From the moment she was on the pony's back and felt its warm coat beneath her, she was at ease. Gripping with her knees she relaxed into the animal's gait, keeping her hands low, holding the rope, and leaning forward. Johnny glanced back at her, then he yelled something, urging his pony on. Tess's pony increased its speed, too, and she felt the wind tugging at her hair as they cantered towards the gate.

As both ponies slithered to a halt, Tess was laughing out loud at the joy of it. She got off and flung her arms round the pony's neck. 'Thank you,' she whispered, breathing in the heady scent of its sweat.

Mike caught them up. He was grinning.

'You done much riding?' he asked.

Tess shook her head. 'I've never done it before.'

Mike let out a whistle. 'What? You never rode before?'

'I've always wanted to,' she added shyly.

Mike said nothing and opened the gate. Johnny dismounted and the boys led the two ponies into the field. Tess followed them in.

As Mike and Johnny took the halters off, Tess stood awkwardly by.

'What are they called?' she asked.

'These two? The one you rode's called Molly. And Johnny's is called Bobby.'

Tess pointed to the chestnut. 'And what's she called?'

Mike scratched the back of his neck. 'Dunno. We ain't had her long.'

Tess was about to say what she called the pony, but the expression on Mike's face stopped her. His eyes had narrowed and he was frowning.

'You were at that meeting up in the village.'

It was a statement, not a question. Tess blushed. 'Yes,' she said quietly.

'Thought I'd seen you before. What's your name?'

'Tess,' she said. Mike turned away.

'I'll check the water,' he muttered and began to walk off.

'Thanks for letting me ride,' she said.

Mike stopped and looked back at her.

'You got a feel for the horses, Tess. Come again if yer like.'

'Can I?'

Mike shrugged. 'Up to you. But if you want to ride, you can help with them, groom them, pick out their feet and that. So long as you don't get in the way.'

Tess was still smiling when she reached home.

Five

Whenever she could sneak away, Tess went to the site. If Mike or Johnny were there, she'd help groom the ponies, getting the tangles out of their long manes and tails and the 'feathers' which covered their feet.

Most times they'd let her ride Molly and she'd canter round the field with Mike on one of the other ponies, racing each other. She fell off a few times, but she never minded. But her favourite was still the bright chestnut mare, the one she called

Flame, and she always took special care with her, brushing her until her coat shone.

But it was getting difficult at home, pretending to Mum and Ben that she was going to Sophie's or Tara's, and pretending to the girls that she had to stay home. She got a scare once when Ben told her that she smelt like a farmyard, and after that she kept a special set of clothes for her visits to the site, changing out of them in the garden shed at home and hiding them under some plastic sheeting.

One day, when she and Mike were fooling about, riding round the field, she noticed a man leaning over the gate staring at them. The man shouted at Mike and Mike immediately cantered over to him. Tess pulled Molly up and waited at the other end of the field. The man seemed angry and he was pointing at her. Then he walked off.

Mike rode his pony back to Tess.

'Who was that?' she asked.

'Me dad,' said Mike.

'He doesn't like me riding here, does he?'

Mike didn't answer. He jumped off his pony and started to take off the halter.

'Shall I stop coming?' asked Tess. 'Are you in trouble?'

Mike shrugged. 'Nah. Dad's just … ' he trailed

off. Then he looked up at her. 'He don't trust outsiders, that's all.'

'I'm sorry.'

Mike sniffed. Then he grinned. 'He'll come round,' he said. 'He's seen how you look out for the horses.'

'He's *seen* me?'

'Yeah. Everyone knows you come here.'

'Everyone?'

'All the families.'

Tess looked shocked. 'I didn't … I didn't realise.' She slipped off Molly's back and set her loose. 'Mike?'

'Yeah.'

'Tell me about your family.'

Mike frowned. 'Wot sort of question's that?'

'Well. You've got a sister, haven't you? I saw her … at that meeting.'

Mike rounded on her angrily. 'Great welcome we got there, didn't we? Soon found out what the village thinks of us.'

Tess nodded. 'We're not all like that,' she said quietly.

But most of them are.

Mike sighed. 'Not surprising we keep to our own, is it?'

Tess shook her head. They were silent for a while, then she went on. 'Your sister, will she come to school next term?'

He shrugged. 'Dunno. Yeah, I suppose.'

'What's her name?'

'Lizzie,' he said shortly.

'Are you all related. All the families on the site.'

'Pretty much.'

'Are you and Johnny related?'

'Yeah. We're cousins.' Mike put his hands in his pockets. 'What's with all the questions, you nosey gorger kid?'

The holidays were over. Tess had been really careful about her visits to the site, but even so she could hardly believe that she'd managed to keep them secret from her friends and family. But maybe it wasn't so surprising. If people from the village saw her riding her bike down the road to the site, they'd think she was going to see her mum at the Tech.

Would she be able to keep riding Molly, keep visiting the ponies? It would be much harder in term time.

At school, everything had changed. She and

Sophie and Tara were in Year Six and their form tutor was Mr Hardy. And there were several children from the site in their form, too. Lizzie, Mike's sister, was one of them.

Tess didn't approach her at first. They stuck together, the gypsy children, not trying to make friends. They were all behind in their studies and had a woman who worked with them to help them.

'Thick as planks, all of them,' said Sophie, tossing back her long fair hair.

Tess's temper flared. 'Well you'd be thick if no one gave you a chance,' she snapped.

Sophie raised an eyebrow. 'Sor-reee!'

Without Mr Hardy's determination, the gypsy children would never have become a part of the class, but he paired them off with the other children whenever he could and encouraged them to work on projects together.

Several times, Tess had tried to talk to Lizzie, but each time Lizzie had turned away from her. Then, one day, Mr Hardy paired them up and they were forced to speak to each other.

'You're Mike's sister, aren't you?' said Tess.

Lizzie raised her eyes and looked at Tess. 'And you're the gorger horse girl,' she replied.

'Gorger' was a word Tess had often heard down at the site and she knew it meant 'outsider', non-gypsy. She nodded, smiling. 'I've liked helping with the horses,' she whispered.

Lizzie didn't answer. She was fiddling with her pen, doodling on the blank sheet of paper in front of her.

Tess looked round the classroom. Mr Hardy was going from group to group, trying to encourage the gypsy children to work together with the others.

Tess and Lizzie had been asked to write something on Ancient Greece. It wasn't difficult. Tess had already done lots on Ancient Greece in Year Five and they had plenty of reference books, but when Tess started to talk about it, Lizzie seemed to close up; she stopped listening and bent her head to go on drawing on her pad.

When Lizzie raised her head from her pad, Tess stole a look at what she had drawn on it.

'Hey, that's really good.'

Lizzie's lips twitched in what could have been a smile.

'If I do the writing, could you draw a picture to go with it?'

Quickly Tess found a few pictures in the books. 'Look. If you draw one of these – then this and this,' she pointed to illustrations, 'then I'll write the words to go with the drawings,' she said.

'I'm no good at words,' said Lizzie.

'And I'm rubbish at drawing,' said Tess, smiling.

After ten minutes or so, Tess looked up briefly from her work. Lizzie was the only gypsy child engaged in what she was doing, her head bent, her tongue protruding slightly from her lips as she concentrated. The rest of the gypsy kids were restless, looking about the classroom, fidgeting, ill at ease and their helper was going from one to the other trying to get them to concentrate.

When the bell went for the end of the lesson, Lizzie was still working. Mr Hardy came over.

'Lovely work, Lizzie. Do you want to finish it at home?'

Lizzie jerked her head up. 'No,' she said, shortly. Then she passed the paper to Mr Hardy, scraped back her chair and hurried across the classroom to join her friends.

At breaktime, Tess hung out with Sophie and Tara.

Tara pointed over to the group of gypsy children who stood in a huddle at the far end of the yard.

'It's weird having them here,' she said.

'What do you mean?' said Tess.

'Well, I dunno, they're so *different*.'

'They wouldn't be so different if you bothered to get to know them,' said Tess.

'OK then,' said Sophie. 'If you're so keen, why don't you go over and talk to them.'

Tess clenched her fists. 'OK. I will.'

She walked slowly over to the group who watched as she approached them. Lizzie whispered something to the others.

They weren't exactly friendly but they all knew who she was and she was able to talk about the horses at least. When the bell went and Tess walked back to her friends, one of them shouted 'Bye gorger horse girl.'

'What's that mean?' asked Tara.

'Haven't a clue,' said Tess, quickly. But she knew it wouldn't be long before her secret was out.

Six

After that, Mr Hardy often paired Tess up with Lizzie. At first, Lizzie didn't talk much, but as they got to know each other better, Tess started asking questions.

'Where did you live before?'

'On other sites. Last one was in Norfolk.'

'Did you go to school there?'

Lizzie fiddled with her hair. 'Yeah. For a bit.'

'Did you like it there?'

Lizzie frowned. 'The kids weren't friendly.'

Tess sighed. She could imagine what that meant. Taunting her, calling her names, refusing to play with her. There'd been a bit of that here, but Mr Hardy had soon put a stop to it. And when two of the traveller children had lost their bags and they'd been found in the bins, Mr Hardy had found out who had done it and gone to see their parents.

'But it's OK *here*, isn't it?'

Lizzie shrugged. 'Yeah. It's OK. ' She fiddled with the pencil she was holding. 'But it's hard.'

'What's hard?'

Lizzie sighed. 'Reading and that. '

Tess' didn't answer. She knew Lizzie was struggling. But then she'd been moved from one school to another. It wasn't surprising she hadn't learned much.

She also knew that Mike and Johnny had started at the secondary school in the next village. Ben had told her that there were some gypsy kids in his year. He also said they often didn't come in.

'How are Mike and Johnny getting on at school?' asked Tess.

'They don't say much,' said Lizzie. Then she changed the subject. 'You coming down to the site at the weekend?'

Tess nodded. 'If I can get away.'

Lizzie looked at her. 'You ain't told yer family, have yer? You ain't told them you come and ride the ponies.'

Tess shook her head. 'Mum would stop me coming.'

Lizzie still held her gaze. 'Why's everyone so scared of us?'

Tess thought of all the whispers that went round the school, the cruel words she'd heard.

'I'm not scared of you, Lizzie. I like you. And I like Mike and Johnny. They've been good to me, letting me ride and stuff.'

Lizzie smiled. 'Our Mike, he loves his horses, don't he?'

'He's great with them. He's got a real way with them. What about you, Lizzie, do you like them?'

'I like them well enough,' she said.

Later that day, Tess was with Sophie and Tara.

'You're getting very cosy with that Lizzie,' said Tara.

'Next thing you'll be down at the gypsy site playing with them,' said Sophie.

Tess blushed and looked away.

'Tess, *have* you been there?' said Tara. Then, when Tess didn't reply, 'Is that where you went in the holidays, when you said you had to stay home?'

Tess hung her head. 'I wanted to tell you,' she began.

'What are thinking of, Tess? I bet your mum doesn't know. She wouldn't let you.'

Tess jerked her head up. 'Please don't tell her. She'd go mental.'

'And I wouldn't blame her,' said Tara.

'But why do you go down there?' asked Sophie.

'I know why,' said Tara suddenly. 'It's the horses, isn't it. You've been down there to be with the horses.'

Tess nodded. She didn't tell them about the riding, or about Mike and Johnny.

'You should have told us,' said Sophie. 'We're your friends. We would have understood.'

'But you shouldn't go down on your own, Tess. We'll come with you next time.'

But Tess knew that wouldn't work. If Sophie and Tara came with her it would ruin everything. The trust she'd built up with Mike and Johnny – and with Lizzie – would be blown away in a moment.

It was really hard to get away that weekend. Kate took Tess to buy some new shoes, then they had to go and pick up Ben from footie practice and call in on the parents of one of his friends. It was late afternoon when Tess said, 'I'll just pop over to Sophie's for a bit.'

Kate looked at her watch. 'Don't be long, love.'

Tess jumped on her bike and pedalled away.

This time, when she reached the field at the back of the site, Lizzie was there, her arms resting on the gate, looking at the ponies. There was no sign of Mike or Johnny.

'They've gone out working with me dad,' said Lizzie.

Tess tried to hide her disappointment. She didn't dare ride if they weren't there. 'Doesn't matter. I'll top up the water and groom Flame.'

'Flame?'

Tess laughed and pointed towards the chestnut mare. 'It's just what I call her.'

'It's a good name for her.'

Tess started to open the gate, but Lizzie put her hand on her arm.

'Leave it, Tess. '

Tess turned round, surprised.

'Come up to the van with me. I've told Mam about you. She'd like to meet you.'

Suddenly Tess felt shy. She looked down at her hands. 'You sure?'

Lizzie nodded. 'Yeah. They all know about you.' She nudged Tess in the ribs, 'Gorger horse girl.'

They walked together through the site. Everyone greeted Lizzie and one or two even raised their hands to Tess, too. Though she got a few silent stares as well.

Lizzie's family lived in a big van in the middle of the site. As Tess and Lizzie approached, the door of the van opened and a woman stood in the entrance. She was dressed in a skirt and a high necked shirt and, even if Tess hadn't recognised her from the meeting, she'd have known she was Lizzie's mum. They had the same black curly hair and high cheekbones.

Tess mounted the steps into the van behind Lizzie. She had no idea what to expect, but when she saw the inside of the van, she gasped. It was immaculate. Every surface was clean and there was decoration and sparkle everywhere. And on one of the walls there were shelves completely filled with china.

'It's beautiful!' said Tess. 'It's like a palace.'

The words had just slipped out, but they broke the ice and Lizzie's mum smiled at her.

It was quite crowded inside, but everything seemed to have its place.

At the end of the van there was a table with seats round it and an old woman was sitting at the table, sewing. She looked up when the girls came in, but pursed her lips and said nothing. She was tiny, her face was very lined and her grey hair was tied back from her face. Lizzie nodded towards her.

'That's my nan,' she said. Me dad's mum.'

Lizzie and her mum talked very fast and some of the words were unfamiliar to Tess, even though she'd picked up some words of the Romany language by listening to Mike and Johnny.

Sometimes, Lizzie's nan joined in, but mostly she kept quiet, although once, when the other two were silent, she said. 'Our Lizzie says you are good to her at that school.'

Tess nodded shyly. She watched Lizzie and her mum lay out tea things on the table – bought stuff, cakes and biscuits Kate would never let her have at home. When it was ready, Lizzie went to the door and yelled and two younger children came in from playing outside, their eyes wide as they stared at Tess.

Later, Mike came in, grabbed a piece of cake and went out again. He grunted a 'Hi' to Tess. And later still, Lizzie's dad arrived. As soon as he came in the van, the chatter stopped; it was as if the rest of them were waiting to see how he would react to Tess. He didn't smile at her, but he nodded in her direction and the women all seemed to relax again.

Tess felt shy in their company and she only spoke when someone asked her a question, but she enjoyed looking round, taking in the way everything had its special place and watching Lizzie's nan as she continued with her work after tea, her nimble fingers sewing more and more sequins on to a bright pink top.

She lost track of time and when she looked at her watch at last, over an hour had passed. Carefully, she wriggled out of her place around the table.

'I'm sorry. I'd better go. Mum will be expecting me home,' she said.

At the door, she said thank you to Lizzie's mum.

'Come and see us again, Tess.'

Tess smiled. 'I'd like that.'

Seven

Tess was late home that evening, and as she wheeled her bike up the path, Kate opened the front door.

'Tess, I *told* you not to be late. I was getting really worried. I was just about to ring Sophie's mum.'

Tess looked down to hide the blush which crept up her cheek. Thank goodness she hadn't rung Sophie's mum. She felt really bad as she mumbled 'Sorry.'

I should tell her. But I've been lying for so long. She'll be mad at me; she'll stop me visiting the site.

The next day was Sunday and Tess tried to be specially nice to her mum. She got up early and made breakfast, then took a tray up to Kate's room. She passed Ben on the stairs as he was making his way out for an early footie practice.

He grinned at her. 'What's all that about?' he said, pointing at the tray.

Tess frowned. 'Thought I'd give Mum a treat, that's all.'

'Huh! You just want something, don't you? What is it – make-up, designer trainers?'

Tess didn't bother answering.

Kate stretched her arms above her head and yawned.

'Thanks, Tessie, that's lovely of you.'

They had a relaxed Sunday together. Ben was out for most of the day and Tess and Kate just pottered round the place. Tess did some homework and Kate spent time weeding in the garden.

'You sure you don't want to go and see your friends?' asked Kate after lunch.

Tess shook her head. 'No, it's nice being here with you,' she said.

Tess took a deep breath. She would tell Kate now. It seemed a good moment.

'Mum ... ' she began.

But then Kate's mobile rang. Tess knew immediately that it was Dad. Kate tensed up, her relaxed mood gone in an instant. When she switched off the phone, she said flatly, 'Dad wants you to go there for half term.'

The moment had passed.

The next day at school Tess caught up with Lizzie at break.

'Thanks for tea on Saturday,' she said. 'It was great. I loved your van.'

Lizzie smiled. 'Yeah. Mam works hard keeping it nice. But it ain't easy for her with the little 'uns and working and that.'

'Where does she work?'

'At the Tech. She's a cleaner there.'

Tess bit her lip. 'My mum works there, too. She's the receptionist. Do you think they know each other?'

'Doubt it,' said Lizzie. 'Mam only works there evenings.'

Sophie and Tara walked over and Lizzie melted

away. 'Lizzie, don't go,' began Tess, but she had already joined the other gypsy kids.

Tara watched her retreating back. 'Have you told your mum about going down to the site?'

Tess shook her head. 'I tried to, yesterday, but ... '

'But what?'

Dad rang and she got in a bad mood.

'Well, you'd better do soon. You can't keep using us as an excuse.'

'What do you mean?'

'Me and Sophie. Saying you were with us when you're down there playing with your gypsy friends.'

Tess reddened. 'You don't even know them,' she shouted. 'You don't give them a chance.' She nodded across at Lizzie. 'You never even try to be nice to them.'

Tara grabbed Sophie by the arm. 'Come on, Soph. She doesn't want to be with us any more.'

Tess felt the tears welling up. 'Course I do ... I ... '

But Tara and Sophie were walking away, leaning in towards each other, giggling.

Lizzie had been watching from across the yard and when the bell went for the end of break, she caught up with Tess as they were going back into class.

'You can come to tea any time,' she said. 'Mam liked you – and Dad says you ain't bad at riding – for a gorger.'

Tess smiled. 'You're kidding me! Did he really say that?'

'Yeah. He don't say much, but he sees a lot.'

It was getting harder for Tess to spend time with the ponies. Harder to think of excuses – and then the evenings were getting shorter, drawing in.

She went for tea at the van several times, though. Once, Lizzie was there alone with her nan. Her mum was out.

It was one of the happiest times Tess had spent there. Lizzie's nan – *Little Nan*, they called her – had lived through so much change. She started telling Tess about how she lived when she was young. Tess watched her face come alive as she described her travels and the rhythm of the seasons. But she often had to rely on Lizzie to translate. Little Nan used so many words that Tess didn't recognise.

'Slow down, Nan,' laughed Lizzie. 'Tess is a gorger, she doesn't know our language.'

'Sorry, sorry, sorry!' The old lady's brown, arthritic hands flew to the side of her head.

Nan talked about how she and her family had travelled round the country in their covered, horse-drawn wagon, (or *vardo*, as she called it) working in the fields, picking hops, potatoes, peas and other vegetables. She spoke of the parties round the fire, with singing and step dancing. And of the winters, making things to sell to the house dwellers.

'What sort of things?' asked Tess.

She replied, talking rapidly and excitedly.

Lizzie translated. 'Wooden pegs, bunches of heather, fresh flowers, fortune telling, Christmas wreaths, wooden flowers.'

'Wooden flowers?'

Lizzie nodded and said something to her nan. Nan reached behind her and pulled something out of a cupboard. She handed it to Tess.

It was a beautifully carved wooden flower on a delicate stem, painted in bright colours.

'It's amazing,' said Tess.

Nan shrugged. 'No call for them now, nor the rest,' she said. 'No moving round neither.'

'You'll start on the Christmas wreaths soon, though, won't you Nan?'

Her nan nodded and smiled.

As Tess was leaving, Nan handed her the wooden flower. 'For you, dearie,' she said.

'Thank you,' said Tess. She wanted to say more, but she felt choked up as Nan smiled down at her.

'You'll do orright girl, I can tell.'

'Watch it, Tess. She'll be telling your fortune next,' said Lizzie.

Tess grinned. 'Not sure I want to know it,' she said.

Eight

It was almost dark as Tess biked back up to the village. She thought about Lizzie's nan and all the changes she'd seen. Did she miss the travelling life, moving on through the seasons, from place to place? Did they all miss it?

But all thoughts of Lizzie's nan were driven from her mind when she got home. As soon as she walked in the door, Kate confronted her.

'Is it true, Tess?'

Tess felt a horrible sinking feeling in her stomach

and her heart started to beat wildly in her chest.

'Is what true?'

Kate turned to Ben, who was sitting in the kitchen, hunched over a mug of tea.

'Tell her Ben. Tell her what you heard.'

'That you're a gypsy lover, that you've been down the site playing with some gypsy girl and riding their horses.'

Tess turned on him. 'Who told you that?'

'Your charming friend Mike,' he said.

For the first time, Tess noticed the cut on Ben's cheek and the bandage round his hand. Ben saw her looking.

'Yeah! That's what your friend did to me.'

'Well, if you got into a fight with him, I bet you started it,' said Tess.

'Just a minute, Tess,' Kate interrupted. 'Are you saying it's true? Are you telling me you've been sneaking off to the site, lying to me about where you were?'

Tess hung her head. 'Sorry Mum, I know I should have … '

Kate put her hands on her hips. 'I can't believe you would do this!'

'You don't understand, Mum. They've been really kind, and … '

'Oh, I understand very well young lady. You found out they had ponies and you decided to make friends with them. When will you ever stop this stupid obsession, Tess?'

'Mum … ' Tess began.

But Kate was on a roll. 'I forbid you to go there again, Tess. Do you understand? We know nothing about these people and I don't want you getting involved.' She turned round and got something out of the oven. When she had straightened up, she said, 'And you are grounded for the rest of the term, do you hear? You don't leave this house on your own. Do you understand?'

'Yes,' whispered Tess.

She saw Ben's stupid grin and she couldn't bear it. She ran upstairs, the sobs breaking out even before she reached her bedroom. Then she flung herself down on her bed, clutching the wooden flower to her chest.

The next morning at breakfast, Tess was pale and hardly spoke.

'It's for your own good, Tess,' said Kate. 'We don't know anything about them.'

Tess opened her mouth to reply, but before she

could say anything, Kate said quickly, 'There's been a whole lot of copper cabling stolen. It's been on the radio.'

Tess frowned. 'So?'

Ben popped another piece of toast in the toaster. 'Great, isn't it. You lovely mates have nicked the cabling and now the whole village is offline.'

'Why are you so sure its them?'

Ben shrugged. 'Stands to reason, doesn't it? They're up to all sorts of dodgy stuff.'

Tess didn't wait to hear any more. She grabbed her school bag and ran towards the door.

'Calm down, Tess. Don't rush off,' shouted Kate.

Tess yanked open the front door. 'What? You going to stop me going to school now, are you?' She slammed the door behind her.

At school, everyone was talking about the theft of the copper cabling and everyone was saying that the gypsies at the site had stolen it.

'One of them's a scrap dealer. Bet they took it. You get a lot of money for copper.'

'They should never have come here. They're nothing but trouble.'

Only Mr Hardy remained neutral. He was taking assembly that morning and he addressed the whole school.

'I want to make it clear that no one knows who stole the cabling and I don't want you accusing anyone until we know some facts. Meanwhile,' he went on, 'we shall have to cope without some of our technology.' He paused. 'And maybe that's not such a bad thing.'

There were groans all round. 'But Sir! How are we going to do our work?'

Mr Hardy smiled. 'People managed just fine before the internet came along. It won't do you any harm to use pencils and paper.'

Tess didn't have a chance to speak to Lizzie until break. Despite some dark looks from Sophie and Tara, she headed over to the group of gypsy children.

'Lizzie. I've been grounded. Mum found out I'd been coming to the site. ' She hesitated. 'I'm sorry.'

One of the gypsy boys overheard. He looked at Tess and then spat on the ground.

Lizzie rounded on him. 'Stop that!' she said. 'Tess ain't like the others. She's my friend.'

Then she turned to Tess. 'Mam and Nan, they'll miss yer.'

Tess felt the tears welling up. 'I want to come again, but Mum and Ben … '

'Hey,' said the boy who had spat. 'You Ben's sister?'

Tess nodded.

'My brother says that Ben's a bully.' Then he walked away, kicking a stone along the ground.

The other gypsy children drifted off, leaving Tess and Lizzie alone.

'They're saying it was me uncle that stole the cabling.'

'Has he got the scrap yard?'

Lizzie nodded. 'But he's legit. He'd never do sommat stupid like that. Why would he? He wouldn't want the village against him.'

'It's not fair,' said Tess.

'No. 'Specially as I reckon we know who did it.'

Just then, the bell rang for the end of break and they had to go in. They trailed into the art room together.

'Who,' whispered Tess. 'Who d'you think did it?'

Lizzie looked around. 'Not here. I'll tell you later. After the art lesson.'

Art was the one subject where Lizzie shone. There was no need for words or spelling or numbers. Here she could relax.

Tess glanced over to look at what Lizzie was painting, the colours swirling around, an image emerging without any effort while Tess struggled, stabbing at the paper.

At last, at lunchtime, they managed to find a place to talk where they wouldn't be overheard.

They were slumped down in the changing room, their backs against the wall.

'Who did it, Lizzie? Who stole the cabling?'

Lizzie sighed. 'I can tell you sommat. It weren't a gypsy.' She examined her fingers, which were still covered in paint.

'But you know who did it?'

Lizzie nodded. 'The men reckon they do. It's a gang run by some bloke who's always trying to get the gypsy lads to do stuff for him.'

'You should tell the police, Lizzie. What's his name, this guy?'

Lizzie smiled at looked up at her. 'We like to keep away from the police,' she said. 'We don't want no trouble. And anyway, no one knows his name – his *real* name. He changes it all the time.'

Tess said nothing and after a while, Lizzie went on.

'It's hard for the lads,' she said.

Tess frowned. 'What d'you mean?'

'They're never gonna earn that much, so it's hard if some dodgy fellow offers them cash.'

Lizzie shifted her position and stretched. 'Me dad never had any education and he doesn't see the point. He just wants Mike to help him with the horses, help out Johnny's dad with the gardening business, that sort of thing.'

'Does Mike want to stay on at school?'

Lizzie shook her head. 'He's having a bad time. He's always fighting and he's not learning much. He often stays home.'

'Does he fight with Ben?' asked Tess quietly.

'Yeah. He says your brother's one of the worst.'

'Ben's an idiot!'

'Doesn't matter what he thinks of Ben. He still likes you. Says you're good with the ponies.'

Lizzie went on, picking at a bit of fluff on her skirt. 'I won't be staying on, neither,' she said quietly. 'Not after this year.'

Tess looked up sharply. 'Why not, Lizzie?'

Lizzie looked at the ground. 'They don't want me going on to the secondary school, mixing with gorger kids.'

Tess frowned. 'But you mix with us here, at primary school.

'That's different.' She blushed. 'At big school it's different … you know, talk about going with boys and that. They think that older gorger girls are fast.'

'That's a bit harsh, isn't it?'

Lizzie shrugged. 'They don't like their ways.'

Tess thought of some of the girls she'd seen from the local secondary school, hanging round with boys, skirts short, full-on make-up. Then she thought of Lizzie's close-knit family, with their age-old customs that she was only just beginning to understand.

'But what will you do?'

Lizzie sighed. 'Mum has to work. Dad hates her going out to work, but he's not making much. She's bin offered more work next year, so they'll need me to mind the little 'uns and do the cleaning and cooking and that.'

'Don't the little ones go to nursery?'

Lizzie shook her head. 'No, we don't hold with that. We like to keep the little ones close.'

'But Lizzie, you're brilliant at drawing. You should go to art college or something.'

Lizzie smiled. 'I couldn't have a career. It's not for the likes of me.'

Tess held her by the shoulders. 'It *so* is! You don't need to be a brilliant speller to do brilliant pictures!'

Lizzie wriggled out of her grip and Tess let her hands drop. She frowned. 'Aren't there school inspectors and stuff? Won't you have to go to school?'

Lizzie shook her head. 'The council lets us do home education.'

'What's that mean?'

'I dunno. I think a teacher comes to the site or sommat.'

It was time to go into afternoon lessons. As they got up, Lizzie suddenly gripped Tess's arm.

'I got a really bad feeling about that guy,' she said.

'What guy?'

'The guy I told you about. Him who runs the gang.'

Tess stopped. 'When you say you've got a bad feeling, do you mean … ?'

Lizzie nodded. 'I see things sometimes,' she said quietly. 'Like Little Nan. And I think there's going to be big trouble in the family because of him.'

Nine

It was half term and Tess had to go to visit Dad and Emma. Ben was supposed to be going too, but at the last minute some lad was ill and Ben was asked if he'd like to go on an elite footie coaching week.

'Trust Ben to get out of it,' muttered Tess, as she slumped in the front seat of the car and waited for Mum to fasten her seat belt.

'Don't be like that, Tess. It's a real chance for him. And Dad understands.'

'Dad always understands if it is about *football*.'

Tess wasn't just cross about Ben, she was fed up at being banned from going to the site – and falling out with Sophie and Tara.

They drove off, Tess sulking and Kate trying to be cheerful but, as they got closer to Dad's house, Tess saw Kate's shoulders tense as she hunched over the wheel.

Just before they got there, Kate said. 'Tess, try and make an effort when you're with them, will you? *I* can put up with your moods, but it's not fair on Dad and Emma – and the baby.'

Tess rounded on her. 'Why do you *think* I'm moody?' she yelled, the tears beginning to well in her eyes. 'You stop me doing the one thing I enjoy and you stop me seeing my friends at the site.'

'Tess, love … '

'I *know* what you're going to say, Mum: "it's for the best. We don't know them. They're gypsies. You can't trust them." Well, you don't know *anything*. You've never met them, you don't even try to get to know them.'

Kate tried to speak, but Tess interrupted her.

'And you've never even met Lizzie. She's lovely. She's brilliant at art and she's pretty and funny and … '

Kate took a breath and glanced over. 'OK,' she said. 'Why don't you invite Lizzie over?'

Tess rubbed her eyes and sniffed. 'D'you mean it?'

'Yes. When you get back, we'll have her over for tea – if she's allowed.'

'We'll make it when Ben's out – yeah?'

Kate smiled. 'Probably best,' she said.

Nothing much had changed with Dad and Emma, except that baby Tom had got bigger. He was staggering around now, and getting into every drawer and cupboard. It took him a while to remember Tess, but soon he was smiling and gurgling at her and putting his arms out to her for a cuddle. Tess held him tight and sniffed his baby smells. 'You're the only good thing about my life,' she whispered.

The day after she arrived, Dad announced that he'd taken time off work and that he had a surprise for her.

Tess was pleased he'd bothered to take time off, but she wasn't that excited about the surprise. It would probably be going to some sport or other, which she'd have to pretend she enjoyed.

But after tea that night, Dad sat back in his chair, bouncing Tom on his knee, and smiled at her.

'Want to know about my surprise?' he asked.

'Sure.'

Dad looked across at Emma. 'It was your idea,' he said. 'You tell her.'

'There's a riding school not far from here, Tess. We've booked you in for a few lessons.'

'It's an early birthday present,' said Dad.

'Wow!' said Tess. She really, really hadn't expected that. She flung her arms round Emma. 'Thanks,' she said. 'That's awesome!'

They went over the next day. The lady at the riding school lent Tess some boots and a hard hat.

'Have you done any riding before?' she asked.

'Sort of,' said Tess. 'But only bareback.'

The lady looked surprised. 'Bareback!'

'Yeah,' mumbled Tess. She wasn't going to tell this woman about her visits to the site.

At first, Tess was mounted on a ploddy little pony and they went round and round in circles with the rest of the class. There were lots of kids there, being half term. They practised rising to the trot and sitting up straight and holding the reins right. It came easily to Tess and, although she loved being with horses again, it was boring. She thought about the bareback races she and Mike and Johnny had had in the field and the lane at the site.

At the end of the lesson, the lady took her aside. 'You're coming again, Tess, is that right?'

Tess nodded.

'Well tomorrow, if you come later, I'll put you in a more advanced class.'

'Really?'

'Yes. You're a natural. And I could see you were bored going round in circles.'

Tess smiled. 'A bit.'

The next day was much better. Tess had a lively pony and she and the other more experienced riders were doing some jumping. At first over little cavaletti poles, then by the end of the lesson over bigger jumps. Tess loved it. It was easy with a saddle and bridle and she instinctively went with the rhythm of the pony and adjusted its stride when they approached the jump wrong.

She'd done a bit of jumping before, bareback over logs. This was a lot easier.

When Dad came to fetch her, she was flushed and smiling.

'Did you enjoy yourself?' he asked.

She nodded. 'It was great.'

The riding school lady came up to them. 'She's

got real talent,' she said. 'It's a shame she's not here longer. She's a natural.'

Tess blushed, but inside she was bursting with pride.

She went twice more to the riding school and each time was better than the last. On the final day she took some carrots to give to the pony she'd been riding, and when she dismounted and took him in to his stable, she took the carrots from her pocket and stroked his neck as he ate them from her hand.

'I shall miss you,' she whispered.

'And we'll miss you, Tess.'

Tess jumped. She hadn't heard the lady come into the stable behind her.

'You know, you should keep on with your riding. Is there somewhere back home … ?'

Tess shook her head. 'There's a riding school in the next village, but Mum could never afford the lessons,' she mumbled.

And now I'm never going to be able to ride the ponies at the site again.

The lady patted Tess's shoulder, then she went out into the yard and Tess saw her talking to Dad.

Ten

Tess's eleventh birthday was coming up.

'Do you want to ask Sophie and Tara over?' asked Kate.

Tess shook her head.

'Have you fallen out with them?'

'No.'

I'm not going to tell Mum about it.

'Well you don't talk about them like you used to.'

Tess turned on her. 'And I can't go and see them, can I, 'cos I'm grounded, remember?'

Kate opened the fridge and got out some pasta. 'I've got a special birthday present for you,' she said.

Tess didn't answer.

Her birthday was the next Saturday. There were cards from her gran and from Dad and Emma – and even a stupid one from Ben. But nothing from Kate.

'We'll have to get in the car to find your birthday present from me,' Kate announced, smiling, but that's all she would say.

It wasn't until the afternoon that they left the house.

'Where are we going?' asked Tess.

'Secret. Wait and see.'

It wasn't far. Just to the next village, where Kate drove down a winding lane and stopped outside a farm gate.

'Mum!' Tess could hardly breathe. The riding school!

'Jump out then and open the gate,' said Kate, smiling.

Tess hesitated. 'But Mum, you can't afford ... '

Kate took her hands off the wheel. 'No, you're

right. I can't afford riding lessons – but that lady you met when you were with Dad, she's been in touch with the woman who runs the place here.'

'And?'

'Well, I'm paying for the lesson today – that's your birthday present – but if she thinks you're any good she's prepared to teach you, if you will help round the place.'

'What! Teach me for nothing?'

Kate fiddled with a strand of her hair. 'No, not for nothing, but a lot less than normal.' She gave Tess a shove. 'Go on, open that gate or we'll be late.'

At the riding school they met Angie, the owner. She had a gruff voice and at first Tess was a bit scared of her. Angie handed her a hard hat and then put her up on a bay gelding called Brandy. They all walked over to the indoor school.

'OK Tess, trot him round the school for me.'

It was just like when she'd been at Dad's. As soon as she was on top of the pony, she felt at ease, at one with him, and relaxed.

Angie watched her carefully as Tess did exactly as she was asked – walking, trotting and cantering, and every time they stopped, she bent down and patted Brandy's neck.

Angie came up to her. 'How much riding have you done?'

Tess looked at Mum. 'Er … lots of bareback riding,' she said.

'Done any jumping?'

'A bit.'

The lesson was over far too soon, but Tess knew she'd done well. She could feel it. And she couldn't stop smiling.

'Right, take his tack off in the stable. Rub him down and we'll turn him out in the field later.'

Tess did as she was told, and when she came out of the stable, holding the saddle and bridle, Angie took it from her.

'Right,' she said. 'I've had a word with your mum. If you want, you can come down here on Saturday afternoons after normal lessons are finished, have a lesson in the covered school then muck out and feed and water for me, clean the tack and such.'

'Can I, Mum?'

Kate nodded.

As they drove home, Kate glanced across at Tess. 'Happy?'

Tess nodded. 'Thanks, Mum.'

They were quiet for a bit, then Kate said, 'I didn't realise how much it meant to you – the riding.'

Tess grabbed her chance. 'Mum?'

'Umm.'

'You know you said Lizzie could come over?'

Kate's hands tightened on the steering wheel. She nodded, frowning.

'Well, what about tomorrow – for tea – if she's allowed? Ben's out, isn't he?'

'I … ' Kate hesitated.

'Please, Mum. You promised. And you'd love her.'

Kate nodded. 'OK. Phone her and see if she's allowed. If that's really what you want.'

Tess let out a long sigh. 'This is my best birthday – EVER!'

She got out her phone. But it wasn't until later that evening that Lizzie got back to her. She sounded nervous.

'Mam says I can, Tess, but what about your brother. Will he be there?'

'Ben? No he's always out on Sunday afternoons at some stupid football thing.'

'Good.'

Tess frowned at the phone. 'He's pretty dumb, but he's not a monster, Lizzie.'

'No, I know. It's just that … '

'What?'

'There's been more trouble with him and our boys at school.'

Tess suddenly felt a tiny lurch of dread.

'What sort of trouble?'

'I dunno. Ben's been calling them names and I think they've been fighting again.'

Eleven

Kate jumped when the doorbell went. She looked at Tess.

'It's OK, Mum, I'll go,' said Tess, running down the hall to the front door.

Lizzie came in slowly, looking about her, seeing the jumble of coats in the hall, the crowded surfaces.

Kate smiled at her. 'Come into the kitchen, Lizzie.'

Lizzie didn't speak at first and Tess talked all the

time, trying to ease any tension, but then, gradually, Lizzie started to relax. Kate had made some chocolate bownies and she bit into one.

'This is great,' she said, wiping chocolate from her lips. 'Mam never makes things like this.' She looked round the kitchen. 'Mostly she cooks stuff in the microwave.'

Kate smiled. 'Tell me about your home, Lizzie. Tess says it's beautiful.'

Lizzie took another bite. 'Our van? It's OK I suppose, but there's not much room.'

'But it's ever so neat and tidy,' said Tess.

Kate grinned. 'Certainly not like our house, then! How do you keep it so tidy if you have to sleep and eat in it any everything? And where do you keep all your clothes?'

Lizzie shook her head. 'We don't eat in it that often. Every pitch has its own day room.'

'It's like a little lounge,' said Tess, 'with a telly and chairs. And there's a kitchen and shower room, too.'

'So you just sleep in the van, then?'

'Me mam and dad sleep in the van, and the two little 'uns. But me dad built sheds on our pitch, behind the van – one for me and one for Mike. That's where we sleep.' Lizzie wiped her mouth with the back of her hand. 'There's ain't much room in them neither, so I don't have many clothes.' She grinned. 'Not like Tess and the other girls at school.'

'But I suppose there was even less room when you were … ' She tailed off.

'When we were on the road? Yes, I guess so. But we've bin settled a long time. You want to talk to my nan about when *she* was travelling.'

'She's told me all about it,' said Tess. 'How they travelled all over, following the work in the fields in the summer, and how they cooked outside on open fires.'

'It sounds so romantic,' said Kate.

Lizzie laughed. 'Oh, my nan loved the roaming and the moving on all the time. But it was hard in winter time. I think she likes being settled now, so long as the family's round her.'

'You've got a big family, have you, Lizzie?'

Lizzie nodded. 'We're all related, like, on the site. Cousins and that.'

'It must be great to be surrounded by your family.'

'They're a pain sometimes,' said Lizzie, 'but we like being all together. My mam says family's everything. When things get bad, you can always count on your family.'

Tess thought of her own family. She hardly ever saw her grandparents or her uncles and aunts, or even her dad. She looked at Kate, who was stirring her mug of tea and staring thoughtfully into it.

'Me mam says you can come and visit if you want,' said Lizzie.

Tess held her breath.

Kate looked up. 'What, *me*?'

'Yeah. She's fond of Tess. She'd like to meet you.'

Kate smiled at her. 'I'd like that very much,' she said slowly.

It was nearly dark by the time Lizzie came to leave.

'I've got to go and pick up Ben,' said Kate to Lizzie. 'I'll drive you back.'

Later that night, Tess sat on the edge of her bed and hugged herself. She couldn't believe it. Mum had met Lizzie, she'd really liked her ('what a lovely girl,' she'd said) and she'd agreed to go to the site the next weekend to meet Lizzie's mum.

When Ben heard that Lizzie had visited, he yelled at Tess.

'You're an idiot! You don't want to get friendly with them. They're thieves, the lot of them, they're nothing but trouble.'

'Ben,' said Kate evenly. 'You don't know that. Lizzie's a lovely girl … '

'Oh not you too, Mum! You've been taken in by them. They fight and they cause trouble – and what about all that copper wiring? Have you forgotten that we were offline because they stole that?'

Tess remembered what Lizzie had told her about the police crawling all over the site. 'The police never found any proof Ben, and Lizzie said … '

Ben interrupted. 'That's because they're clever. Clever and sly. They'll have sold the stuff on to some dodgy dealer. And I tell you something else, one day there's going to be a showdown with those boys at school.'

There was no reasoning with him. His mind was made up. As far as Ben was concerned, the gypsies were the enemy.

The following Saturday, Tess and Kate visited the site together. They didn't tell Ben where they were going.

'I feel bad about Ben,' said Kate.

Tess took her hand. 'Don't worry, Mum, he's just being a teenager.'

Kate laughed out loud. 'I suppose. But I don't like deceiving him.'

'We'll tell him when we get home.'

Lizzie's mum greeted them at the door to the van. Kate had been tense as they'd walked through the site, but as soon as she saw Lizzie's mum she smiled.

'Oh, it's *you!*' she said.

Lizzie's mum turned to Tess. 'You never told me your mum worked at the Tech. I've seen her there.'

'No, I … ' Tess blushed. She should have realised that they might have met.

They went inside the van and Kate gasped. 'It's amazing,' she said. 'Everything so tidy and clean. And look at all that beautiful china.'

Lizzie's mum smiled. 'That was my mam's,' she said. 'It's always passed down from mother to daughter when a girl gets married.'

Lizzie's nan was sitting there, working on some Christmas wreaths. Tess hadn't seen her for a while and she looked much frailer, but her knobbly hands never stopped weaving.

Kate and Tess admired the wreaths. 'They're beautiful,' said Kate. 'So many berries.'

Lizzie's nan smiled. 'Yer need to gather the holly early,' she said. 'Before the birds get to the berries.'

The visit went much better than Tess had

expected. As they got up to go, Lizzie said. 'Why don't you come and see the horses?'

Tess looked at Kate. Kate smiled. 'Sure,' she said.

The three of them walked out of the site and down the lane which led to the field. As they approached, Tess saw Lizzie's dad leaning over the gate watching Mike and Johnny riding a couple of the ponies in the field. She hesitated.

'Is it OK?'

Lizzie nodded. 'Don't worry. Dad'll be OK.'

He turned round as they approached and nodded to Tess. 'This is my mum,' she said. He nodded again but said nothing.

For a few minutes, they all stood in silence at the gate, watching the boys, then Mike rode over. He jumped off his pony and led it over to Tess.

'Want a go?'

Tess glanced over at Lizzie's dad. He nodded at her. 'You get up there gel and show your mum what you can do.'

Tess climbed over the gate and let Mike give her a leg up onto the pony, then she gathered the rope halter in her hands, squeezed the pony's flanks with her knees and she was off, galloping round the field, her hair flying.

Kate gasped and put her hand to her mouth.

Lizzie smiled. 'She won't fall. She's a really good rider,' she said.

At last Tess came back. She slid off the pony's back and patted his neck.

'I've missed you,' she whispered.

Lizzie's dad cleared his throat. 'She rides like a gypsy girl,' he said. Then he turned to Mike. 'We should take her to a horse fair.'

Kate's eyes widened.

'The horse fairs are great,' said Mike. 'There's all sorts goes on. The trots, the bareback riding.'

Kate said nothing, but Tess was certain she'd not be allowed near any horse fair.

Twelve

It was the last day of term and Tess had brought Christmas presents for Sophie and Tara. When she gave them their packages, suddenly things were all right again, especially when Lizzie handed them both a Christmas wreath.

'Hey,' said Tara, turning the wreath round in her hands, 'this is great. It'll look brilliant on our door; much better than the plastic thing Mum bought. Where did you get it?'

'My nan makes them,' said Lizzie.

'Wow!' said Sophie. 'That's amazing.'

Tess smiled to herself.

Later that day, she said to Lizzie, 'Thanks for doing that – giving Soph and Tara the wreaths. They were really pleased.'

'I've got one for you and your mum, too,' said Lizzie. 'I'll fetch it later.' Then she sighed. 'I don't know if Nan will be making them next year.'

'What do you mean?'

'I just feel it. Like I told you, sometimes I know when bad things are going to happen.'

Tess put her hand on Lizzie's arm and squeezed it. Then she handed her a parcel. 'Here's your present,' she said.

Lizzie unwrapped it. Inside was a box of paints and some paintbrushes. Lizzie laughed. 'You don't give up, girl, do you?'

Tess smiled.

Christmas was uncomfortable for Tess. They always had to go over to her gran and granddad, and her Uncle Sam and his perfect wife and perfect children always came over, too. It meant that Kate was tense and Ben always stirred things up and made them worse. In the middle of Christmas dinner he suddenly said, 'Tess has got these gypsy friends now.'

There was a horrified silence and Tess immediately got a lecture from Uncle Sam. All the same stuff about how gypsies were thieves and couldn't be trusted, how they were dangerous.

Ben was smirking at her from the other side of the table. Tess felt the blush rising to her cheeks and the tears pricking behind her eyes. Suddenly, she scraped her chair back and flung her fancy napkin down on the table. She faced her uncle. 'You know nothing about them,' she yelled.

Kate stood up too. Gently, she put her hand on Tess's arm. Her eyes were hard. 'No,' she said. 'Tess is right. You don't. I've met her friend and her family and they are lovely.'

Ben snorted and Tess rounded on him. 'They *are*! You don't even know Lizzie. And,' she went on, 'her family are a lot nicer to each other than mine.'

There was a shocked silence and Kate closed her eyes.

They left as soon as they could.

When they were in the car, Kate yelled at Ben '*Why* do you always do that?'

'What,' said Ben, all innocence.

'You know perfectly well what I mean, Ben.

Make a difficult situation a deal worse. It's hard enough without you stirring things.'

She was close to tears.

'Sorry Mum,' said Ben. 'It's just that … why do we have to do it?'

'Do what?'

'Go there every year?'

Kate was quiet for a moment. 'I know, love,' she said at last. 'But they are family.'

'Some family,' muttered Ben. And Tess thought of the big extended gypsy family at the site, looking out for one another.

The rest of the holiday was good, though. Tess was getting on well with her lessons at the riding school, and every Saturday she biked over there. And Kate had finally allowed her to go to the site again.

For the last few days of the holiday, Tess was due to go to Dad and Emma, and this time her dad was coming down to fetch her.

'Are you all packed up, Tess?' Kate was busy tidying the house.

Tess nodded. 'I'm all good. I'm just going to go down to the site and say goodbye to the ponies.'

Kate smiled. 'They'll survive without you for just a few days!'

'Please, Mum!'

'OK. Off you go. But don't be late for Dad. He'll be here by five o'clock and it's nearly four now.'

'OK.'

Tess didn't bother checking whether Lizzie was in. It was already nearly dark when she reached the site, so she went straight to the field. She could make out the shapes of the ponies in the gloaming, and she called out to them.

They trotted over to the gate pushing their noses at her for carrots and apples. She laughed. 'Greedy things, take your turn.'

Then she frowned. Flame, the chestnut mare, was missing. She was always the first to come over. Where was she?

Tess climbed over the gate and walked all round the field, calling softly. There was no answering whinnie.

Tess stood still. She knew the mare was pregnant. Had something happened to her? Had Lizzie's dad taken her somewhere? She frowned. And then she heard it, not far away, the unmistakable sound of distress, heavy breathing, a faint whinnie.

She listened. The sounds were coming from the far side of the field. Tess ran over, but still she could see nothing.

And then she spotted it. A large shape on the ground by the shelter.

'What is it girl, what's the matter?'

Tess knelt beside the heaving body. She stroked Flame's head and she could feel the heavy sweat on the animal's neck.

This isn't right. She's in trouble.

It was much darker now. Tess climbed over the gate and ran back to the site and to Lizzie's van. As she was about to knock she heard the sound of angry voices inside. She hesitated, but then she thought of the mare. Even if she made a fool of herself, she didn't care. She banged on the door.

The voices stopped immediately. She heard someone coming and she braced herself.

Lizzie's dad was there. He looked angry.

'What do you want?'

'I'm really sorry,' began Tess. 'But it's Flame.'

He frowned. 'What?'

'Flame. The chestnut mare. She's … well I think she's in trouble.'

Lizzie's dad suddenly gave her his full attention.

'What's the matter with her? Is she foaling?'

Tess nodded. 'Yes. But ... but I don't think ...
I don't think it's coming.'

'Wait there!'

He went inside the van again and emerged
wearing boots and an old coat and carrying a big
torch.

'Come on, then!'

Tess didn't dare disobey. She walked beside him.
He yelled over his shoulder. 'Mike! Johnny! Mare's
in trouble. Bring the rope and hurry on down to the
field.'

When they reached the field, Lizzie's dad shone
his torch on Flame.

'You're right, lass,' he said, then he handed the
torch to Tess. 'Here, shine this on her rear while I
take a look.'

When he straightened up, he grunted. 'Not
good.'

Mike and Johnny arrived with the rope. Tess
continued to hold the torch as steady as she could
while the man and the boys wrestled to release the
foal. They managed to get the rope round the foal's
tiny legs but it wouldn't budge.

'She's breathing funny,' said Tess.

'Here, hold this and don't let go,' said Lizzie's
dad, handing the rope to Mike, then he crawled

round to the mare's head. As Tess kept the light steady, he examined Flame's eyes and put his hand on her neck. Then he felt in his pocket and brought out a small bottle.

Tess swallowed. 'Should I phone the vet?' she asked.

He didn't bother answering. But Mike muttered, 'Vet don't know no more than Dad.'

'Hold that light real steady, Tess.' It was the first time he'd called her by her name and she felt a thrill of acceptance as she watched him put the contents of the bottle into a syringe and then squirt it into the side of the animal's mouth.

He patted her. 'Easy, lass. That'll help with the pain.'

He turned to the boys. 'We'll wait a bit then try again.'

They huddled there in silence as the minutes ticked by. After a while, he checked Flame's breathing. 'Right,' he said. 'We'll give it another go.'

Tess hated watching the heaving and pulling, but she never let the light waver.

'It's coming, Dad!' said Mike.

'Gently now.'

The mare strained again and Tess could sense her weakness.

Lizzie's dad talked gently to her. 'All right, lass. Not long now.'

Tess held her breath as the boys and the man pulled on the rope again.

'Steady! Not too hard.'

And then, at last, with one last shudder and strain from the mare, Tess saw the slithering mass of the foal separate from its mother and land on the grass.

Immediately Mike freed the little thing's nose. Flame tried to stagger to her feet, but she was too weak and Johnny carried the foal round to her where she licked at its fur.

'It's alive!' said Johnny.

Tess looked on, shaking with cold now. 'What about Flame?' she asked.

Lizzie's dad didn't answer. He was at the mare's head now, gently trying to persuade her to stand. And at last she did.

'She's that weak,' he said to the boys. 'We'll put them in the shelter. '

'Will she be all right?' asked Tess.

He turned to her. 'I doubt she'll have another foal,' he said. Then he put a hand awkwardly on Tess's shoulder. 'But if you'd not called me, she would have died and the foal along with her.'

Thirteen

Tess had heard her phone ringing while she was with the mare, but she'd turned it off. Nothing else seemed important. Any thought of the time, the darkness, her dad, had gone from her head. She switched it on just as they were leaving the field and it rang immediately.

'Mum, look I'm sorry ... '

'Tessa. Where the *hell* have you been? I've been worried sick and your dad's furious. What *were* you thinking of?'

Mum only called her Tessa when she was really angry.

'I'm on my way.'

Lizzie's dad was close by. 'I'll give you a lift in the truck,' he said.

She smiled. 'Thanks.'

He chucked her bike in the back of the truck and they drove off, bumping down the track and out onto the road. In no time they were at Tess's door.

She jumped out and was about to run inside when she heard a car door slam.

'What's this, Tess?' Her dad's voice. He must have been waiting for her outside.

Probably had another mega row with Mum, thought Tess.

Tess, caught off guard, stumbled over her words. 'Sorry Dad, I was … I was helping with the mare.'

Her father said nothing but he stared at Lizzie's dad, who dumped the bike on the verge, got back in the truck and drove away. As the truck roared up the street, Dad grabbed her arm.

'Who was *that*?'

Tess didn't answer. She shook off his arm, ran up the path, went inside the door. She grabbed her bag from the hall, shouted goodbye to Mum then came back and got into Dad's car.

But he wouldn't let it alone. As they were driving along, he kept going on about it, about how Mum hadn't been honest with him, how she'd not told him about Tess being friendly with gypsies.

In the end, Tess burst into tears. Dad stopped the car in a layby and turned to her. 'Sorry love, I didn't mean to upset you. It's because I'm worried. I don't want you seeing those people.'

'You don't even *know* them,' snapped Tess. 'You're as bad as Ben.'

Her time with Dad and Emma was strained. Tess sulked and even little Tom couldn't cheer her up. Dad took her to the riding school once, but the owner was away and the person in charge made Tess ride round in circles with the beginners, so even that was no fun.

When term began again, Sophie and Tara gradually started to talk to Lizzie.

'That wreath you gave me,' said Tara. 'My mum loved it.'

Sophie joined in. 'Everyone asked where we'd bought ours, and I told them about your nan making them.'

Lizzie just smiled, but both she and Tess could sense the difference.

'They ain't so scared of me now,' said Lizzie.

And one day Sophie said to Tess, 'You're right. She's lovely.'

'Yes,' said Tess simply. 'She is.'

But, in the second week, Lizzie came late to school and Tess could see that she'd been crying. During the first lesson, Tess kept glancing at Lizzie, whose head was bent over her book.

At break, Tess caught up with her in the yard. 'What's the matter, has something happened?'

Lizzie smoothed back her dark curls. 'It's Nan,' she said, and immediately her eyes welled up.

Tess moved closer and put her hand on Lizzie's arm. 'Is she ... '

Lizzie sniffed. 'She's dying, Tess.'

'Oh Lizzie!'

'She's that frail now. And she's took to her bed.'

'She might get better.'

'No.' Lizzie shook her head. 'No, she won't ... I've seen ... '

'What?'

'Like I said, I've got the gift, like she has. We both know.'

'The gift?'

'Seeing things that are going to happen.'

The next day, Lizzie wasn't at school. Tess rang her in the evening.

'Nan's worse,' said Lizzie. 'She'll not last the night.'

'Can I ... would you like me to come ... ?'

'No. Thanks. We're all with her, Tess. The family. We'll stay with her till she goes.'

Lizzie was right. Her nan died that night.

Tess knew the family wouldn't want her around, but the next weekend she went to the field to check on Flame and her foal. He was a healthy little thing, with his bottle brush tail and long gangly legs. He'd be light legged, like his mum. Tess tried to get close to him, but he shied away and she had to be content with stroking Flame's nose.

'Clever girl.'

Tess felt a surge of love for the pony and just thinking that she'd saved her and her foal, made her feel proud.

As Tess walked slowly away, back up the path, she saw that there was smoke rising up from the site. She peered through the hedge and saw Lizzie's dad and some of the boys stoking a bonfire close to Nan's van.

She remembered Lizzie telling her that when a

person dies, the Romany gypsies burn all their possessions.

Her nan had had very little. It wasn't a big bonfire.

She watched for a while, thinking of Nan and her skill at making the Christmas wreaths. And of all the stories she told of her time as a young girl, when she travelled up and down the country, working in the fields in the good weather and making things to sell when it was cold, of meeting up with friends and family and of music and laughter round the open fire.

She remembered Nan telling her about the beautifully painted vardo her father owned. 'Where is it now?' Tess had asked and Nan had looked surprised. 'Why child, burned, of course. All gone. When me dad died, we burned the wagon. It was the way things were.'

Surely they wouldn't burn Nan's van?

Lizzie came into school the next day. 'We're having Nan's body brought back to her van,' she said.

'What?'

'Just for the night before the funeral.'

Tess felt awkward. 'Oh.'

'She was fond of you, Tess.'

'I was fond of her, too.'

'Would you like to come and say goodbye to her?'

Tess hesitated, scared. 'Do you want me to?'

Lizzie nodded. 'And Mam and Dad would like it, too.'

So, after school, the Friday before the funeral, Tess and Lizzie went back to the site together.

Nan's little van was surrounded by family, going in and out.

Lizzie squeezed Tess's hand. 'We must never leave her alone,' she said. 'Come on, we'll go in now.'

It was gloomy inside the van. Lizzie's mum was there and some other woman Tess didn't know, and they were both talking quietly to Nan as though she was still alive.

Nan's body was laid out in an open coffin in the middle of the van and there were lighted candles at her head. She looked very peaceful – and so tiny. Lizzie bent over the body and talked to her, too, then she gestured to Tess.

'Do you want to say goodbye?'

Tess had been scared before, but suddenly it seemed the most natural thing in the world to talk to Little Nan, say goodbye and say thank you for all her kindness and her stories.

The next day was Saturday – the day of the funeral. Tess had promised that she and Kate would follow the coffin as it left the site. Tess had thought that there would be a car – a hearse – for the body, and both she and Kate were taken aback when they saw a magnificent glass-sided coach being drawn by four black horses with plumes on their heads.

As the procession wound its way from the site and towards the local church, all the mourners followed on foot. Nan's family had come from all over the country to say goodbye to her and there were vans on the verges everywhere: all down the side of the road leading up to the site, in the lane, even round by the field.

There weren't many people Tess knew among the mourners, but she spotted Mr Hardy and she saw him later, again, after the funeral, talking to a group of gypsy boys.

Fourteen

After the funeral, Tess kept away from the site, sensing that the family didn't want outsiders around. Lizzie didn't come into school for a few days and Tess phoned her.

'Is everything OK?'

There was a pause. 'Yeah. Yeah, it's OK, Tess. I'll be back soon. I can't talk now.'

Tess ended the call, frowning. She'd heard noises in the background, voices raised in anger.

When Lizzie finally appeared, she walked into

the classroom late, looking tired. Tess whispered. 'What's been happening, Lizzie? What's up? Why haven't you been at school?'

Lizzie pushed her hand up into her black curls. 'It's bin hard since Nan died.'

'Stop talking, you two,' said their teacher.

It wasn't until break that they could talk properly. Lizzie sat down, her back against the wall.

'I've bin looking after the little 'uns. Mam's had to take on more cleaning work.' She didn't look at Tess. 'The funeral cost a lot,' she said, then, when Tess kept quiet, she went on. 'Everyone helped – all the relations and that – but … ' She tailed off.

'What about your dad's work?'

Lizzie sighed. 'Not too good,' she said. 'There's no gardening work around this time of year and he can't sell horses 'til the Spring and … well, he gets mad that Mum's bringing in the money, not him. Then he takes a drink and … '

Tess thought back to the shouting she'd heard when she'd been to fetch Lizzie's dad from the van, the night the foal had been born.

'I wish I could help,' she said.

Lizzie smiled. 'You're listening to me. That's a help.'

For the next few weeks, Lizzie only came to school every now and again, and when she did she always looked tired. Tess went to visit the ponies, but she only went up to the van once. Lizzie's dad was there and, although he said nothing, she could sense the tension.

Then, towards the end of term, Lizzie started to come more regularly.

'Dad's gone up North,' she said. 'To his brother's scrap yard. He's got him work up there for a few weeks.'

'So things are better?'

Lizzie smiled. 'For now.'

'What about the little ones?'

'My aunty's taken to minding them when Mam's not there.'

'Can I come and see you again then?'

'Yes. Mam would be pleased. And Dad said if you want to help more with the horses, he'd be grateful. He knows you have a way with them.'

Tess couldn't believe it. 'Your dad said that?'

Lizzie nodded. 'He may be rough, me dad, but there's a soft side to him. He loves his horses.'

So Tess resumed her visits to the site and to Lizzie's van. One day, she noticed that Nan's van had gone.

'It hasn't been burnt has it?' asked Tess. Lizzie laughed. 'No, that was only in the old days, when all the wagons were wooden, they'd burn them once someone died, so their spirit was freed. Now we sell them on as soon as we can.'

The evenings were getting lighter now and Tess could visit the ponies more often. She worked hard caring for them, and for the first time she realised how much there was to do. Mike helped, but Johnny came less and less, now that his uncle wasn't around to make him.

Flame and her foal were thriving, but Mike was gloomy about them.

'She's a pretty thing all right,' he said, nodding at Flame. 'But Dad says another foal would kill her, so he won't sell her. He don't want no new owner trying to put her in foal.'

'So you'll keep her?'

Mike shrugged. 'Dunno.'

After seeing to the ponies, Tess walked up towards the van. She felt she could go there again, now that Lizzie's dad was away. Lizzie was sitting outside, huddled against the sharp March wind. She looked up when Tess approached.

'You OK?' asked Tess.

Lizzie took her arm and steered her away from

the van. 'I'm that scared, Tess. I must tell someone.'

'What? What are you scared about?'

Lizzie hesitated. 'You know I told you that I have the sight, like me little nan?'

Tess nodded. 'Have you *seen* something? Something that's going to happen?'

Lizzie held tightly onto Tess's arm. 'It's about Mike and Johnny. Something bad's going to happen to them. I can feel it. I have these awful dreams.'

Lizzie looked so scared and worried; Tess tried to reassure her.

'It's just a dream, Lizzie, that's all. A nightmare.'

'No, you don't understand. It's not a dream. It *will* happen. I *know* it will happen.

It turned out that Lizzie was right to be worried. Two nights later, Mike and Johnny were caught breaking into a big house in another village and all the trust that had been built up over the past months between the travellers and the rest of the community was shattered.

'What did I tell you?' said Ben, when the news broke. 'They're nothing but trouble, those two.'

Lizzie stayed at home until Tess persuaded her to come into school again.

'It's not your fault, Lizzie. No one blames you.'

Lizzie shook her head. 'You know why they did it, Tess?'

'Because money is short?'

Lizzie nodded. 'They thought they could help. Earn a bit of easy money. It's that man I told you about, the one who runs the gang. Apparently he offered them a load of cash.'

'Oh Lizzie, I'm sorry!'

'And the stupid boys got caught, didn't they.'

'Can't they tell the police about this man?'

Lizzie looked at her. 'Huh! The police won't take no notice of two thieving gypsy boys, would they? And anyway, the guy's disappeared. But there's one good thing.'

'What's that then?'

'They've bin let off with a caution. They ain't gonna be locked up.'

'That's good.'

'Yeah. One of the policeman, he's one of us. He was a big help.'

When Lizzie came back to school, Tess walked in with her and soon Sophie and Tara joined her. There were whispers, of course, and some horrible insults thrown at her, but Mr Hardy soon put a stop to them.

He helped the boys deal with the police, too, and spoke up for them, promising to try and find apprenticeships for them at the Tech.

Their families gave them a hard time, too. Lizzie's dad came back from the North and decided to take Mike back with him.

'There's plenty of work up there for now, boy. No need to thieve.'

Then he came to Tess's house, driving up in his old truck.

Fortunately, Ben was out. Kate answered the door. For a moment there was an awkward silence, then Lizzie's dad cleared his throat.

'Is the lass there?' Tess had seen him and she hurried up the hall and stood beside Kate. 'Is something wrong?' she asked.

'It's the ponies, lass. I'm taking Mike up North for a few weeks.'

Tess knew immediately what was coming.

'I'll help care for them,' she said.

He smiled. He so rarely smiled, and his face was completely changed. Suddenly he looked less scary. 'Just keep an eye on them until we get back.'

He hesitated, finding it hard to say what was on his mind. 'You know what to do – and I know you care for them,' he muttered. Then he turned to

Kate. 'She's got a rare touch with horses,' he said.

Fifteen

During the holidays, Tess was at the site most days, except when she was at the riding school. Everyone at the site knew her now and she moved freely among the vans, greeting people by name. Johnny wasn't that interested in the horses and she hardly saw him, but one day she bumped into him in the lane.

'Hi,' said Tess.

Johnny didn't answer. She'd heard Ben say he'd not been at school much last term.

'You going back to school after the holidays?'

Johnny shrugged. 'Nah. I'd rather help me dad.'

Tess frowned. 'I thought Mr Hardy was looking at getting you an apprenticeship at the college.'

Johnny scowled. 'You mind yer own business, kid.'

Tess blushed. She was quite scared of Johnny, but she needed to ask him something. She took a deep breath. 'I've had an idea about Flame.'

'Yeah?'

'You know your uncle said she's no good in the trotting cart – too nervy?'

He nodded. 'He don't know what to do with her and that's the truth.'

'I think she could be a jumper.'

Johnny frowned. 'We never have jumpers. The trots and the bareback riding, that's what the ponies do.'

'Do you think your uncle would mind if I brought someone round to look at her, see what they think?'

'Who's that, then?'

'Angie. The lady from the riding school.'

Johnny frowned again.

'She's really nice.'

'I dunno. You'd better ask me uncle. Give him a ring. I can't say.'

Tess smiled to herself. Then she went to Lizzie's plot and told her and her mum of her plans.

'I think it's a great idea, love,' said Lizzie's mum. 'I don't have anything to do with the horses. You know that. But he's grateful you're looking out for them. He was worried to leave them to Johnny. Johnny don't have the same feel for them – not like Mike.'

'Phone him tonight, when he gets in,' said Lizzie. She grabbed her phone to give Tess the number.

That evening Tess got up her courage and made the call. When he heard her voice, Lizzie's dad sounded anxious. 'What's wrong, girl?'

'Nothing. The horses are fine.' Then she told him of her plan.

There was a long silence. Then at last –

'A jumper, you say?'

'I know the little one's not weaned yet, but if I could lunge Flame over poles, just see if she has it in her, then, when you sell her foal … '

'And this woman from the riding school? Would she want paying?'

'No,' said Tess. 'She wouldn't need any money.'

She hadn't even asked Angie.

There was another long silence. 'You do what you think right, girl.'

Tess came off the phone and punched the air. 'Yeeessss!'

The Travellers
Four people, one story

Rosemary Hayes lives in Cambridgeshire with her husband and an assortment of animals. She worked for Cambridge University Press and then for some years she ran her own publishing company, Anglia Young Books. Rosemary has written over forty books for children in a variety of genres and for a variety of age groups, many of which have been shortlisted for awards.

Rosemary is also a reader for a well known authors' advisory service and she runs creative writing workshops for both children and adults.

To find out more about Rosemary, visit her website: **www.rosemaryhayes.co.uk**

Follow her on twitter: **@HayesRosemary**

Read her blog at **www.rosemaryhayes.co.uk/wpf**